parents

8/21

Bulwell		
2 2 FEB 2022		
3 0 JUN 2022		
2 6 OCT 2022		
2 0 NOV 2023		

Nottingham City Library & Information Service

You can renew your books online
or by phoning or visiting the Library

Nottingham
City Council

52000

Summary: "A young child asks his mother about other nursing mammals and their young."

First Paperback Edition

Mama, Who Drinks Milk Like Me?

Melissa Panter

Mama, does Little Bat drink his mama's milk like me?

□ □ □

Yes, very much like you. And he will drink other bat mamas' milk if he needs to!

(Sometimes even human babies drink other mamas' milk for different reasons.)

Mama, when will Little Hedgehog stop drinking his mama's milk?

□ □ □

When he is able to find bugs and berries to eat before the winter comes.

(You may eat berries, but probably not any bugs!)

Mama, does Little Kangaroo have to share her mama's milk?

□ □ □

Yes, Little Kangaroo will share her mama's milk with a newborn brother or sister.

(Isn't sharing nice? What things do you share?)

Mama,
when will Little Giraffe stop drinking his mama's milk?

□ □ □

When he is big enough to defend himself from lions and hyenas.

(Good thing we don't have any hyenas in our backyard!)

Mama, where does Little Hippo drink her mama's milk?

□ □ □

Sometimes Little Hippo drinks her mama's milk under water.

(I don't think that's something that we'll try!)

Mama, does Little Elephant drink his mama's milk like me?

□ □ □

Yes, and just like you, he'll stay close to his mama for a very long time.

(Little Elephant also hugs like you; except he uses his trunk!)

Mama, when will Little Panda stop drinking her mama's milk?

□ □ □

When she can eat tough bamboo and sleep in tall trees all by herself.

(Do you think you would like to sleep up in a tree like Little Panda?)

Mama,
how much milk
does Little Whale
drink?

□ □ □

Little Whale drinks so much
milk that it could fill more
than two bathtubs every day!

(That's quite a lot more than you drink!)

And Mama, when will Little Walrus stop drinking his mama's milk?

□ □ □

When Little Walrus is big enough to eat clams and swim around the arctic all by himself.

(Brr! That sounds very cold!)

But Mama, when will I stop drinking Mama's milk?

□ □ □

When you and I choose, little one.

(And even after that, you will always have special together time with Mama.)

CPSIA information can be obtained
at www.ICGtesting.com
Printed in the USA
BVHW091734060421
604325BV00010B/965

9 781320 702966